D0624105

DOES A DINOSAUR CHECK YOUR TEETH?

Text copyright © 1995 by The Child's World, Inc.
All rights reserved. No part of this book may be
reproduced or utilized in any form or by any means
without written permission from the publisher.
Printed in the United States of America.

Library of Congress Cataloging-in-Publication Data

Woodworth, Viki.
Does a dinosaur check your teeth? / Viki Woodworth.
p. cm
Summary: Simple, humorous rhymes suggest some of the
occupations that help people in a community.
ISBN 1-56766-178-5
[1. Occupations—Fiction. 2. Stories in rhyme.]
1. Title.
PZ8.3.W893Do 1995   94-45829
[E]—dc20   CIP / AC

DOES A DINOSAUR CHECK YOUR TEETH?

Written and Illustrated by
Viki Woodworth

WHITE MOUNTAIN LIBRARY
Sweetwater County Library System
Rock Springs, Wyoming

Viki Woodworth and family.

Whom do you visit when you feel sick?

A toad?

A doctor?

A moose
or a chick?

A Doctor

Who checks to see if your teeth are clean?

A dinosaur?
A pig?

A dentist
or a queen?

A Dentist

Who comes to the rescue when a building is on fire?

A cat?
A firefighter?

A sock
or a tire?

A Firefighter

When you need help, whom should you call?

The police?
A pumpkin?

A sheep
or a ball?

WHITE MOUNTAIN LIBRARY
Sweetwater County Library System
Rock Springs, Wyoming

The Police

In your town or city, wherever you might be,

it takes many people to make up

your
community.